Highlights®
BOOK OF
Birthday
PARTY PLANS

Festive Ideas for Fun-Filled Birthdays

by Colleen Van Blaricom • illustrated by Ron LeHew

Boyds Mills Press

Published by Bell Books
Boyds Mills Press, Inc.
A Highlights Company
815 Church Street
Honesdale, Pennsylvania 18431
Printed in the United States of America

Publisher Cataloging-in-Publication Data
Van Blaricom, Colleen.
    Highlights book of birthday party plans : festive ideas for fun-filled
birthdays / by Colleen Van Blaricom ; illustrated by Ron LeHew.—1st ed.
[48]p. : col. ill. ;   cm.
Summary : Birthday party plans based on themes such as a carnival,
the Olympics, a safari, and more.
ISBN 1-878093-38-X
1. Children's parties. 2. Games—Juvenile literature. [1. Parties. 2. Games.]
I. LeHew, Ron, ill. II. Title.
793.21—dc20   1995   CIP
Library of Congress Catalog Card Number 90-85914

First edition, 1995
Book designed by Charlie Cary
The text of this book is set in 12-point Century Schoolbook.
The illustrations are done in watercolor wash.
Distributed by St. Martin's Press

10 9 8 7 6 5 4 3 2

It's Your Birthday . . .
that most special day of the year

• •

You've been excitedly counting the days until your birthday arrives. You want to have a great party so your friends and family can help you celebrate. Inside this book you'll find lots of fun ideas for a truly special party that you'll always remember.

The parties in this book are easy to plan and don't cost a lot of money. Each party is divided into five parts: **Invitations, Decorations, Menu, Activities,** and **Favors.** You can change the parties around if you'd like. For example, use the star-shaped Sheriff's Badge Cookies from the "Wild, Wild West Party" in your "Blast Off!" party. You can come up with your own ideas, too.

Here are some suggestions to make your party run smoothly:

• Keep the guest list small. A good rule of thumb is to invite one guest for every year of your age (for example, if you are eight years old, invite eight guests). Try to invite guests who are all the same age.

• Keep the party's length at two hours or less.

• Ask your parents, relatives, or friends to help you plan and get ready for the party. It's especially important to have an adult's help when you are cooking or using an appliance such as a stove or a blender.

• Remind your mom or dad to put away any breakable knickknacks, or place gates across areas in your home that kids should steer clear of. Make sure the party area is safe.

• Have everything set up and ready to go before the party starts. Decide on the order of the activities—do you want to play games first and then eat? Do you want to split up the activities and open gifts in between?

• Mail or hand-deliver the invitations two weeks before the party.

• Borrow from other party plans if you think you may need more activities.

• Allow your guests to watch the games if they don't want to take part, or offer them some toys to play with instead.

• Have more food and favors handy in case an extra person shows up.

• Ask someone to take lots of pictures for you.

Hope you have a great birthday!

Fun-in-the-Sun

Whether your party is held at an ocean beach, a lake, or in your own backyard, fun in the sun will be had by all. Have guests bring their bathing suits, sun-block lotion, and beach towels. You supply the "beach," the food, and the games!

Invitations

You will need white paper, a small bowl, a pencil, scissors, and markers. Fold a piece of white paper in half. Trace around the bowl to get the shape of a beach ball. Make sure part of the circle falls on the fold so you can open the invitation. Cut out the circle. Draw sections on the circle, like a beach ball, and color each one a different color. Inside the invitation write "Have fun in the sun at (your name)'s Birthday Beach Party!" Include the date and time of the party (you may also want to mention a rain date), your address, R.S.V.P. and your phone number, and "Please wear your swimsuit!"

Decorations

If your party is at the beach, you won't need any decorations. Just bring beach towels, beach balls, sand toys, and an umbrella or two. If the party is to be held

FOLD

HAVE FUN IN THE SUN AT DANIEL'S BIRTHDAY BEACH PARTY
Where: 912 Fairfax St.
When: Saturday, July 22
2-4 P.M.
R.S.V.P. 555-3941
Please wear your swimsuit!

Beach Party

in your backyard, lay out the beach towels, beach balls, and umbrellas. Fill your sandbox with sand, or bring in a pile of sand for the party. Fill your wading pool with water, or set up a sprinkler or hose.

Menu

Keep the food simple, since you'll be eating outside. Offer the guests sandwiches, potato chips, carrot and celery sticks, and watermelon. Of course, no party would be complete without a cake, especially a Beach Cake. (See recipe, page 6.)

Beach Cake

Bake a sheet cake, using your favorite mix. Frost half of the cake with chocolate icing to make the beach. Frost the other half with blue icing (mix a few drops of blue food coloring into vanilla icing) to make the water. Insert some small paper umbrellas into the beach. Use small rectangular cookies or candies for beach towels and water rafts. Small round candies make good beach balls, or use candy rings as life preservers.

Activities

Keep the activities simple for younger kids: blow bubbles, build sand castles, swim in the water or wading pool (*adult supervision is recommended*), run through the sprinkler or hose, and have a water-balloon toss. Here are some suggestions for more structured activities:

Off and On

The players place beach towels on the ground. A leader yells, "On the towel!" and everyone must jump on his or her towel. Then the leader yells, "Off the towel!" and everyone must jump off. The leader can yell faster and faster, and try to confuse the players by yelling "Off the towel!" or "On the towel!" twice in a row. Players who have not followed the command are out. Play continues until one person is left.

Red Light, Green Light

Before the guests arrive, make two lines at opposite ends of the party area. One person, "It," stands on one line with her back to the group. The rest of the players stand horizontally behind the other line. "It" calls out "Green light!" and the players start moving toward her. Then "It" calls out "Red light!" and quickly turns around. If she catches any players moving, they are out. The game continues until one of the players tags "It," who must chase that player back to the starting line. If "It" tags the player before he reaches the line, that person becomes "It." If she does not tag the player, she remains "It" for the next game.

Sandbox Search

Before the guests arrive, hide pennies or seashells in the sandbox. At the signal "Go!" players can search for the hidden items.

Favors

Guests can take home favors such as sand toys, beach balls, plastic sunglasses, pinwheels, bubble-blowing solution, and kites.

Haunted House

Ghosts moan and witches cackle. Cobwebs dangle in your face. Bats circle overhead. Your guests will have a hauntingly good time.

Invitations

You will need construction paper, scissors, glue, markers, and moveable plastic eyes. Fold a piece of dark-colored paper in half. Cut out a house from black paper. Cut windows and a door in the house,

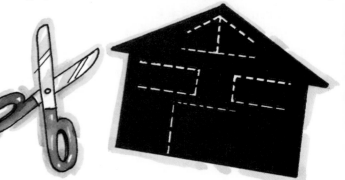

and fold them back, as shown. Glue a piece of white paper to the back of the house. Glue the house to the inside of the card. Using the markers, draw spiders, monsters, and ghosts in the door and windows, and glue moveable plastic eyes on them. Write "Come to (your name)'s Haunted House Birthday Party!" Include the date and time of the party, your address, and R.S.V.P. and your phone number. Cut out half a moon from yellow paper and a bat from black paper and glue it near the house. Cut out a rectangle from yellow paper and write on it "Behind each window you will see a scary creature...EEEEEEEEK!" Glue it to the front of the card.

Decorations

Hang orange and black balloons and streamers around the party area. Cut out Jingle Ghosts (see directions, next page) and black bats, and hang them from the

Party

ceiling. Tape paper skeletons and witches to the walls. Drape black thread or yarn around the party area for cobwebs. Paint or carve faces on pumpkins, and place them around the party area and on the table. Stuff a shirt, pants, and socks with newspaper. Pin them together to form a body, prop it up in a dark corner, and place a pumpkin "head" next to it. Drape a white sheet over the table for a tablecloth. Set a piece of black construction paper and white chalk at each place setting so guests can draw.

Jingle Ghosts

You will need white poster board, scissors, a paper punch, jingle bells, and white string. Cut out a ghost from the poster board. Using the paper punch, punch two eyes in the ghost's head. Punch a hole at the bottom of the ghost's body. Thread a short length of white string through the bell, and then tie it through the hole at the bottom. Punch a hole at the top of the ghost's head, and thread a length of white string through to hang.

Menu

Spooky Sandwiches

Grill one ham and cheese sandwich for each guest. Cut ghosts or monsters from cheese slices and place one on top of each sandwich, as shown. (*You may need an adult to help you with this.*) Place the sandwiches on a baking sheet and keep in a warm oven until party time. Serve with a tray of vegetables.

Scary Ghost Cake

Bake a sheet cake, using your favorite mix. Cut it into a ghost shape. (It may help to freeze the cake before cutting it.) Frost the cake with white icing. Use raisins or chocolate chips for the ghost's eyes.

Witch's Brew

Mix one part cranberry juice with two parts ginger ale. Add a scoop of vanilla ice cream to each glass of punch.

Activities

The Great Ghost Hunt

Before the party, cut out lots of ghosts from white paper, and hide them around the party area. Prizes or treats can be given to players who have found the "most ghosts."

Ghosts and Goblins

Before the guests arrive, mark two lines about 20 to 40 feet apart in the party area. Players form two teams—the Ghosts and the Goblins. The Ghosts stand on one line and the Goblins stand on the other line. The Ghosts turn their backs to the Goblins, who silently sneak toward the Ghosts. When they are within 15 feet of the Ghosts, an adult calls out, "The Goblins are coming!" The Ghosts turn around and chase the Goblins back to their line. Any Goblin who is tagged by a Ghost before reaching her goal line becomes a Ghost and goes back with that group. The last Goblin left is the winner. Next, the Goblins turn their backs, the Ghosts sneak up on them, and so on.

Wrap the Mummy

Players form into teams of two. Each team gets a roll of bathroom tissue. At the signal "Go!" one person wraps his or her partner from head to toe with the bathroom tissue. The team that finishes first is the winner.

Make a Monster

Give each guest a large piece of poster board and a wooden dowel. Fold the poster board in half and draw a monster on it. Cut out the monster. (There should be two.) Place glue on one end of the dowel rod and on the monsters, and sandwich the rod in between them. Provide guests with chenille sticks, markers, construction paper, glitter, fake fur, etc., and let them decorate their monsters. When everyone is finished, have a Monster Parade!

Favors

Guests can take home the monsters they made. Some other suggestions are small plastic monster figures, monster stickers, glow-in-the-dark items, and books about ghosts and monsters.

Blast Off!

Do you love to gaze at the stars? Do you dream of being an astronaut someday? You will think that dream has come true when you step into this party galaxy!

Invitations

You will need poster board, scissors, aluminum foil, glue, orange and red crepe paper, construction paper, and markers.

Cut out a rocket from poster board, and glue aluminum foil to the front of it. Cut thin strips from the red and orange crepe paper. Glue the strips to the bottom of the rocket to look like flames. Cut out a square from construction paper. Using a marker, write "Blast off to (your name)'s birthday party!" and glue it to the rocket. On the back of the rocket, write the party details, such as the date and time, your address, and R.S.V.P. and your phone number.

Decorations

Create a sparkling galaxy by draping white, twinkling Christmas lights around the party area to look like stars. Cut out stars and moons from foil paper and hang them from the ceiling. To make planets, paint or glue glitter on plastic-foam balls and hang them from the ceiling. Lots of silver, blue, or white balloons will add a finishing touch. For moon rocks, paint rocks black, paint a guest's name on each one, and set them on the party table. Set the Rocket Centerpiece (see directions, next page) in the middle of the table.

tube to the square. Stuff the inside of the tube with newspaper. Insert the 3-inch tube into the 4-inch tube and tape them together. Stuff the 3-inch tube with newspaper. Insert the 2-inch tube into that tube and tape together. Cut out a half-circle from the poster board and cover it with aluminum foil. Roll it into a cone shape and tape it shut. Glue the cone to the top of the rocket. Cut out the letters "U," "S," and "A" from construction paper, and glue them to the rocket. Cut out a rectangle from white paper. Use markers to draw the American flag on it. Glue the flag to the rocket.

Menu

Planet Pizzas

You will need one or two cans of refrigerated biscuits (depending on the number of guests), one 8-ounce can of tomato sauce, 8 ounces of mozzarella cheese, oregano, and pepperoni slices. Bake the biscuits according to the package directions. When they have cooled, split each in half. Top with the remaining ingredients. Place on a greased baking sheet and broil them for two to three minutes. *(Watch them to make sure they don't burn. Adult supervision is recommended.)*

Rocket Centerpiece

You will need poster board, scissors, aluminum foil, tape, a ruler, newspaper, glue, construction paper, and markers. Cut a square from poster board and cover it with aluminum foil. Cut three 5-inch squares from poster board. Roll them into three tubes—one 4 inches in diameter, one 3 inches in diameter, and one 2 inches in diameter—and tape shut. Cover all three tubes with aluminum foil. Tape the 4-inch

Moon-Landing Cupcakes

Bake cupcakes, using your favorite mix. Frost them with chocolate icing. Top each cupcake with a small teddy bear cookie and a tiny paper American flag glued to a toothpick.

Activities

Who Is the Pilot?

One player leaves the room. All other players form a circle. A pilot is selected, and that person begins an action, such as clapping. The group copies the pilot's action while the player returns to the room. The pilot continues to change actions, and the group copies him while the player tries to discover who the pilot is. (Make sure to instruct the players to avoid watching the pilot.) When the pilot is spotted, he leaves the room and the game begins again.

Orange-Up

Combine one part orange juice with three parts lemon-lime soda. Add orange slices.

Satellite Salad

Mix up your favorite combination of vegetables, such as lettuce, tomatoes, cucumbers, radishes, carrots, and celery, and top with your favorite dressing.

Astronaut's Bluff

Blindfold one person and spin her around several times, then stop. The other players move around the Astronaut, making sounds while she tries to tag them. The first person tagged becomes the next Astronaut.

Pin the Tail on the Comet

Draw a comet on a piece of paper, and tape it to a door or wall. Cut out one comet tail for each player and put his or her name on it. Put a piece of tape on the back of each tail. Hand the tail to the player, blindfold her, and spin her around. Head her in the right direction so that she can stick the tail on the comet. The guest with the tail closest to the correct position is the winner.

Aliens

Form teams of three players. Give each team one piece of paper folded into three parts. To start, only the top third should be showing. One person draws the head of an alien on the top. Then she flips the paper over, so that only the middle section is showing, and hands it to the second person. He draws the alien's middle on the paper. Then he flips the paper over to the bottom and hands it to the third person. She draws the bottom of the alien. Open the paper to see the wacky alien you've created!

Black Hole

You will need one sheet of white paper for each player and one sheet of black paper for the Black Hole. Tape all the papers to the floor, forming a circle. Each player stands on a sheet of paper. When the music begins, the players march around the circle, stepping from one paper to the next. When the music stops, whoever is standing on the Black Hole is out. That person takes a white sheet with him. Continue playing until one person is left.

Favors

Some favors to give guests are small toy spaceships, small plastic astronaut and alien figures, glow-in-the-dark stars and planets, marbles, balloons, and books with space themes.

Carnival Time!

Food! Games! Prizes! Fun! Who can resist a carnival? Your guests will love to play Go Fish! and Roller Ball and have their fortunes told, while munching on corn dogs and lemonade.

Invitations

You will need construction paper, scissors, markers, ice-cream sticks, and glue. Cut out two squares from construction paper. On one, draw a pointing hand and write "This way to (your name)'s birthday carnival!" Include the date and time of the party, your address, and R.S.V.P. and your phone number. Squeeze glue on the tip of an ice-cream stick and place the stick between the back of the invitation and the other square.

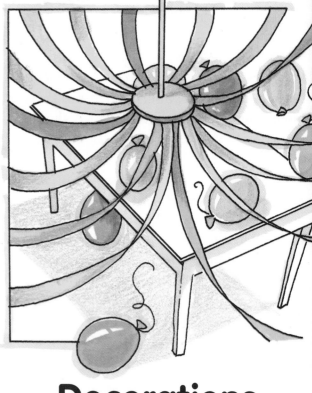

Decorations

If you're holding your party indoors, you can create a big-top swag over your table with colored crepe-paper streamers and tape, as shown. You can make carnival booths out of large appliance boxes. Cut holes for windows, then paint and decorate the "booths." If you don't have any large boxes, set up and decorate tables for your booths. And, of course, no carnival would be complete without lots of balloons.

Menu

You can "sell" the party refreshments from one of the carnival booths. Some suggested treats are corn dogs (see recipe below), peanuts, popcorn, and lemonade.

Corn Dogs

You will need a package of refrigerated corn bread sticks and thirty-two cocktail-size hot dogs. Heat oven to 375°. Separate the corn bread dough into sixteen pieces, then cut each in half. Wrap one hot dog in

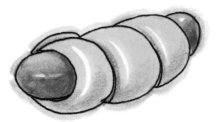

each piece of corn bread. Place them on a cookie sheet and bake for 14 to 16 minutes. Serve the corn dogs with mustard.

After the carnival games you can serve the Carousel Cake (see recipe below) and the Clown Cones (see recipe, page 18).

Carousel Cake

Bake a two-layer round cake, using your favorite mix. Frost the cake with white or pink icing. (Mix one or two drops of red food coloring into white icing to make pink

icing.) Place animal crackers around the side of the cake. Insert eight peppermint sticks around the top edge of the cake. Cut out a circle (11 inches in diameter) from a piece of colored paper. Cut a slit halfway through, overlap 2 inches, and tape shut to make a dome. Place the dome on top of the peppermint sticks. (Dab some frosting on top of the peppermint sticks so the dome will stick to them.)

Clown Cones

Set one paper baking cup on a cookie sheet for each guest. Place one round scoop of ice cream in each cup. Create eyes and a mouth with tubes of icing, nuts, raisins, or chocolate chips. Use a cherry for the nose. Sprinkle the top of the scoop with coconut for hair, and top with a sugar cone and cherry for a hat (secured with a dab of frosting).

Go Fish!

Create a fishing pole using a stick and a piece of string or yarn with a large plastic hook on the end. Guests cast the fishing pole into the booth, and a helper on the other side attaches a prize for them to reel in.

Activities

The games can be set up at the carnival booths or at tables. You can award prizes such as small plastic toys, pinwheels, small stuffed animals, bubble-blowing solution, balloons, or small balls.

Jelly Bean Guess

Fill a jar with jelly beans you've counted and write the total on a piece of paper. Set the jelly bean jar at the carnival booth and provide slips of paper and pencils. Guests write their names and the number of jelly beans they think are in the jar. The guest with the guess closest to the actual total wins a prize.

Face Painting

Ask an adult to paint clown or other faces on the guests, using the following face paint recipe: 2 tablespoons vegetable shortening + 5 tablespoons cornstarch + 1 tablespoon flour. Color with food coloring or with cocoa powder for brown.

Roller Ball

Tape a piece of cardboard to one end of a muffin tin to form a ramp. Fill each cup in the muffin tin with candies or small prizes. Each guest gets three tries to roll a Ping-Pong or other small ball up the ramp and into the muffin tin. If a ball lands in one of the cups, the player may keep the prize.

Marble Drop

Insert four cardboard tubes of different heights in a coffee can. (Each tube is labeled with the number 1, 2, 3, or 4, from tallest tube to shortest tube.) Every guest stands over the can and gets five tries to drop a marble into the tubes. Each marble dropped in a tube receives the score on that tube. The guest with the highest total score is the winner.

Bean Bag Toss

Draw a large clown face on cardboard or poster board. Cut a hole for the clown's mouth (large enough for a bean bag to be thrown through). Prop it up on a chair. Each guest gets three tries to throw a bean bag into the clown's mouth.

Fortune-Telling

Before the party, write a fortune for each guest on a slip of paper. Insert one fortune into a balloon and blow up the balloons. Tie a piece of yarn or ribbon onto each balloon. An adult dressed as a fortune-teller can hand a balloon to each guest. They can then pop the balloons to receive their fortunes. (*To ensure safety, quickly throw away the pieces of popped balloons.*)

Favors

Guests can take home the prizes they won.

Under the Sea

Cruise on a submarine down to your own undersea paradise. You and your guests will sail boats, race sharks, munch on submarine sandwiches and whale cake, and much more. What a whale of a party!

Invitations

You will need construction paper, scissors, glue, and markers. Fold a piece of blue paper in half. For the sky, cut a piece of white paper to fit on the top half of the card. For waves, cut scallops on the bottom of the paper and glue in place. Cut out a sun and a submarine from paper, as shown, and glue on the card. Decorate the card with markers. Write "Come join me on the U.S.S. (your name)..." on the outside of the card and "for a birthday party under the sea!" on the inside. Include the date and time of the party, your address, R.S.V.P., and your phone number. Cut out a submarine, fish, seaweed, coral, and other sea life from paper and glue to the bottom half of the card.

Decorations

Hang green, brown, and blue "seaweed" streamers from the ceiling. Cut out fish from brightly colored paper and hang them from the ceiling. Cut out an octopus, shark, and other ocean life from cardboard or poster board, paint them, and prop them up around the party area. You can also decorate the room with stuffed sea animals. Hang fishnets from the ceiling or walls, and tie seashells and driftwood to them.

For a table centerpiece, fill a fishbowl with water that has been colored blue with a few drops of food coloring. Create a sea scene with plastic fish, a sunken ship, diver, and other characters that can be purchased at a store that sells aquariums.

Menu

Serve Submarine Sandwiches (recipe below) with potato chips and a fruit plate. For the grand finale, serve Mermaid Shakes and Whale Cake. (See recipes, page 22.)

Submarine Sandwiches

Cut French bread or submarine loaves lengthwise. *(Adult supervision is recommended.)* Stuff the rolls with your favorite fillings, such as lunch meats, cheeses, tuna or chicken salad, lettuce, and tomatoes. Slice into sandwich-size portions.

Mermaid Shakes

In a blender, mix two pints of milk with one tablespoon of sugar, a few drops of peppermint extract, a few drops of green food coloring, and one or two scoops of soft vanilla ice cream.

Whale Cake

Bake a sheet cake, using your favorite mix. Frost the cake with white icing. Using blue cake-decorator icing from a tube, draw the outline of a whale on the cake, as shown. If you'd like, fill in the whale outline with blue icing. Use a chocolate chip for the whale's eye.

Activities

Crab Walk

Before the guests arrive, draw or place masking tape as a start line and a finish line in the party area. At the start line, the players crouch down on their hands and feet, with their stomachs facing up. At the signal "Go!" the players race toward the finish line in the crab position. Whoever reaches the finish line first is the winner.

Sardines

This game is played the opposite of Hide-and-Go-Seek. One player hides and the other players search for him. As each player finds the one in hiding, he or she squeezes in with him, like sardines, and stays hidden quietly. The game continues until the last player finds all the rest hidden together.

Fish, Fish, Shark!

This game is played like Duck, Duck, Goose! The players all sit in a circle. One player is "It." "It" walks around the circle, patting the other players on the head and saying, "Fish, fish...." "It" then pats one player on the head and yells, "Shark!" That player must chase "It" around the circle and tag him before he reaches her spot. If she tags "It," he remains "It" for the next round. If she doesn't tag "It," she becomes "It" for the next round.

Windjammer Race

Fill a wading pool with water. Each player gets a small boat to race across the pool. At the signal "Go!" players blow their boats across the pool. The boat that reaches the other side of the pool first is the winner. You can also play this game by blowing Ping-Pong balls across the floor.

Captain Says

This game is played like Simon Says. One person stands in front of the group. That person calls out "Captain says, touch your nose," or some other command. If the leader gives any command *without* saying "Captain says" first, and a player follows the command, that player is out.

Favors

Some suggestions are bubble-blowing solution, plastic sea creatures, seashells, plastic boats, and nautical books or stickers.

Safari Party

You sneak quietly through the tall grass. Look to the right—there's an elephant! Watch out—you're about to step on a snake! Invite your friends to join you on a trip to the deepest rain forests—right in your own backyard.

Invitations

You will need white and brown construction paper, scissors, green yarn, glue, and a green marker. Glue a length of green yarn across the middle of a piece of white paper. Fold a piece of brown paper in half, then in quarters, accordion-style. Draw a monkey shape on the top quarter, as shown. Make sure the monkey's hand is on the right-hand fold. Cut out the monkeys. Glue the monkey chain on the white paper, their hands over the green yarn as if they were swinging on a vine. Using the green marker, write "Grab a vine and swing into (your name)'s Safari Birthday Party!" at the top of the invitation. Include the date and time of the party, your address, and R.S.V.P. and your phone number.

Decorations

Hang green and brown streamers and balloons from the ceiling so that the party area looks like a rain forest. Place lots of plants and stuffed animals around the room. You might even set up a tent if you have one. Decorate the table with an animal-print tablecloth and tableware.

Place bunches of bananas and coconuts in the center of the table for a centerpiece. Set a Snack Cup (see directions below) at each place setting.

Snack Cups

You will need paper nut cups, a roll of green crepe paper, scissors, animal stickers, and glue. Cut three strips of crepe paper to fit around the cup. Fold each one in half, then in quarters. Cut slits halfway down each strip. Open up the strips. Glue the unfringed half of one strip to the top of the nut cup. Glue the second strip to the nut cup, overlapping the first strip. Attach the animal stickers on top of the second

strip. Glue the third strip of crepe paper to the bottom edge of the nut cup so that it partially covers the stickers. Pull the fringe out a little bit so that the animal stickers look as if they're sneaking through the grass. Fill the Snack Cups with treats.

Menu

Serve grilled hamburgers on buns with fixings such as cheese, lettuce, tomatoes, onions, ketchup, and mustard. Serve Safari Sippers (see recipe below) and Banana Pops (see recipe, page 26.)

Safari Sippers

Pour fruit punch into a punch bowl. Garnish with ice cubes and slices of orange, lemon, and lime.

Banana Pops

Insert a wooden stick into each banana. Dip the bananas in vanilla yogurt, roll in granola, and freeze until party time.

Safari Cupcakes

Bake cupcakes, using your favorite mix. Mix a few drops of green food coloring into vanilla icing, and frost the cupcakes. Mix a few drops of green food coloring into coconut and sprinkle on top. "Hide" a small plastic animal in the coconut grass.

Activities

Animal Masks

You will need paper plates, a paper punch, scissors, a pencil, yarn, construction paper, markers, and glue. Punch a hole on each side of the paper plates. Cut eye holes in the plates. Give plates to the guests and let them create their own animal masks using the construction paper and markers.

When they are done, thread yarn through the holes so they can tie the masks to their heads

Animal Charades

Write the names of animals on slips of paper and put them in a container. A guest chooses one of the slips and pretends to be the animal listed on it. The rest of the guests try to guess what animal she is.

Don't Get Entwined in the Vines

All the guests hold hands and form a circle. Two people form an arch (a vine) over the circle. When the music starts, the guests march under the vine. When the music stops, the vine comes down, trying to catch someone. Those caught go into the center of the circle. When there are two people in the center, they form another vine over the circle. The last person to be caught is the winner.

The Tiger's Going to Get You

Mark off two goal lines about 30 feet apart. All the players except one stand on one of the goal lines. The extra player is the Tiger, who stands in the middle. When the Tiger yells, "I'm going to get you!" the players run as fast as they can to the opposite goal. The Tiger tries to tag as many players as he can. Those who are tagged join him in the middle and help him catch the others. The last player to be caught is the next Tiger.

Safari Search

Before guests arrive, hide small plastic animals all over the party area. Guests can go on safari and search for the animals.

Favors

Guests can take home the Snack Cups and the animals they found during the Safari Search. Other ideas are safari hats, boxes of animal crackers, and books or magazines about wild animals.

Olympics Festival

Have you ever dreamed of participating in the Olympics? You can come pretty close with your Olympics Festival—from the opening festivities, to the games, to the awards ceremony.

Note: Although this party is meant to be held outdoors, you can adapt some of the games to be held indoors.

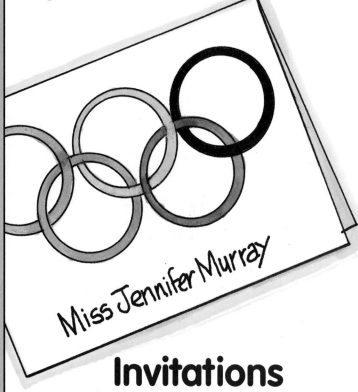

Invitations

You will need white paper and markers. Fold a piece of white paper in half. Using the markers, draw the Olympics insignia on the front of the paper, as shown. Underneath the insignia write the guest's name. You will need to choose a different country for each guest to represent in the Olympics. Inside the invitation write "(Guest's name) is cordially invited to represent (country's name) at (your name)'s Olympics Birthday Party." Include the date and time of the party, your address, R.S.V.P., and your phone number, and "Please wear appropriate clothes for playing games."

Decorations

Decorate the party area with balloons and streamers in the Olympic colors, (blue, yellow, black, green, and red). You can also coordinate the tablecloth and tableware in the Olympic colors. Set a Flag Place Mat (see directions below) at each place setting. Use the Olympics Cake as a table centerpiece.

Flag Place Mats

You will need construction paper, scissors, glue, and markers. First check an

encyclopedia or other source to find out what the flags of different countries look like. Using the paper, scissors, and glue, make a flag for each country that your guests represent. With the markers, write the guest's name and his or her country on each place mat.

Menu

It's best to serve the main meal after the games have been completed, but you might have drinks and snacks available for guests while they're playing.

Olympics Cake

Bake a round cake, using your favorite mix. Frost the cake with vanilla icing. Draw the Olympics insignia on the cake, using blue, red, yellow, green, and chocolate (for the black ring) icing squeezed from tubes.

Sundae Bar

Set up a buffet table with sundae fixings and let guests create their own ice-cream masterpieces. Some suggestions are ice creams; frozen yogurts; sauces such as hot fudge or strawberry; and toppings such as crushed cookies and candies, fruits, sprinkles, nuts, and cherries.

Hero Sandwiches

Cut French bread or submarine rolls lengthwise. *(Adult supervision is recommended.)* Stuff the bread with favorite fillings such as lunch meats, cheeses, tuna or chicken salad, lettuce, and tomatoes. Slice into sandwich-size portions.

Activities

Get your Olympics off to an inspirational start with the Parade of Nations. Guests hold up their Flag Place Mats as they march around the party area to the Olympics theme or other music. You, of course, lead the parade with the torch (orange or red tissue paper "flaming" from a cardboard tube).

Guests then pin their flags on their backs. Let the games begin!

Long Jump

Guests run to the starting line, then jump as far as they can. The guest who jumps the farthest is the winner.

Pillowcase Race

Each guest steps into a pillowcase and hops from the start to the finish line while holding up the pillowcase.

Penny Toss

Line up three bowls about 5, 8, and 10 feet away from the starting line. The bowls are worth 5, 10, and 15 points, respectively. Each guest gets five chances to throw a penny into the bowls. At the end, add up the points. The player with the highest number wins.

Backward Run

Guests run backward as fast as they can from the start to the finish line. *Make sure this race is run on a soft surface!*

Balloon Race

Players line up at the starting line, each behind a balloon. To win the race, a player must get his balloon to the finish line first without using his hands. (Players can use their heads, feet, elbows, and knees, or even blow on balloons to move them along.)

Obstacle Course

Before the guests arrive, set up the course and test it to make sure it's safe. Have a stopwatch ready to time the guests. Here are some suggested "obstacles": Run along a board; jump over a rope or pole; dribble a ball around some chairs; crawl through a large box; balance an egg on a spoon; and run carrying a cup of water without spilling it. The guest with the fastest time is the winner.

The Awards Ceremony

Set up three boxes (preferably of different heights) for the winners to stand on. There is a gold medal, a silver medal, and a bronze medal for the top three winners of each game. Make sure to award medals to guests who did not win any of the games. You can give them awards for "the silliest face," "the best smile," or some other accomplishment. (See medal directions below.)

Favors

The Medals

You will need a one-yard length of ribbon for each medal, glue, cardboard, scissors, gold and silver glitter, and markers. Cross the ends of the ribbon, as shown, and glue. Cut out two small circles from cardboard. Spread one with glue and sprinkle with glitter. On the other, write (Winner's name), (Gold, Silver, or Bronze) Medal for the (name of the event). Glue the glitter circle on top of the crossed part of the ribbon. Glue the other circle to the back of the glitter circle and the ribbon. Some other ideas for favors are balls, jump ropes, visors, and sweatbands.

Tea Party

Little ladies and gentlemen, dress in your finest, and come join us for cakes and tea. You will not *be required to sit stiffly without speaking. You* will *be encouraged to join in the fun and games!*

Invitations

You will need construction paper, a pencil, scissors, glue, and decorations (ribbon, lace, flowers, feathers, sequins, etc.). Fold a piece of construction paper in half. Draw a hat shape on the paper, with the top of the hat on the fold, as shown. Cut out the hat. Decorate. For the suggested wording of the invitation, see the illustration and substitute your own name, date, time, address, and R.S.V.P. and phone number. Hand-deliver the invitations or carefully insert them in an envelope and mail them.

Note: Create top hat invitations for boys and picture hat invitations for girls.

Decorations

Decorate the table with a fancy tablecloth, cloth napkins, napkin rings (see directions, next page), candles, and a centerpiece of

FOLD

Miss Courtney Jackson cordially invites you to a Birthday Party Tea on Saturday, July 27th, at 3:5 P.m. 18 Forest Drive R.S.V.P. 555-0070

flowers. Perhaps your mom or dad or another adult would allow you to use their china and silverware, or you can use fancy paper goods.

Ask two adults to dress up as maid and butler for the party. The butler could announce guests as they arrive ("Presenting Miss Ashley Davidson"). The maid could serve the food to the guests.

Fancy Napkin Rings

You will need cardboard tubes, construction paper, scissors, glue, and decorations (ribbon, lace, flowers, feathers, etc.). Cut a 2-inch section from a cardboard tube. Cover the section with construction paper and decorate. Insert the napkins into the napkin rings and lay one at each place setting.

Menu

Teatime Sandwiches

Cut slices of bread with a heart-shaped cookie cutter. Spread with peanut butter and jelly; egg, chicken, or tuna salad; cream cheese and strawberry jam; or other fillings.

Fruit Salad

Mix together strawberries, blueberries, banana slices, or any other favorite fruit.

Flower-Basket Cupcakes

Bake cupcakes, using your favorite mix. Frost them with vanilla icing. Top the cupcakes with flower-shaped candies. Push one end of a piece of red shoestring licorice into each side of the cupcake for a basket handle.

For beverages, serve ginger ale in plastic punch glasses or herbal tea with milk and sugar.

Activities

Dress-Up Box

Have a box of dress-up clothes available for the guests to use. Some suggestions are dresses, jackets, pants, vests, bow ties, shoes, costume jewelry, hats, purses, feather boas, capes, and gloves.

Suitcase Relay Race

The guests form two teams and stand behind the starting line. At a line about 15 feet away, stand two suitcases full of clothing. (Each suitcase should contain similar articles of clothing, such as a shirt, a pair of pants, a hat, shoes, jewelry, gloves, a belt, and a coat.) At the word "Go!" the first person on each team runs to the suitcase, opens it up, and puts on all the clothing. She closes the suitcase and runs with it back to the starting line. She then removes all the clothing, puts it back in the suitcase, closes it, and returns it to its original spot. Then she runs back to her team and tags the second player in line, who follows the same actions. This continues until every player has had a turn. The team that finishes first wins.

Gossip

All the guests sit in a circle. One person thinks of a message and writes it down on a piece of paper. He then whispers the message to the person next to him. That person, in turn, whispers it to the next person, and so on around the circle, until it reaches the person who sent the message. That person announces the message he received as well as the original message.

Paper-Plate Party Hats

You will need paper plates, paper bowls, scissors, glue, a paper punch, ribbon or yarn, and decorations (feathers, sequins, glitter, fabric scraps, and flowers). Cut out the center of the paper plate. Glue the bowl upside down on top of the paper plate rim. Decorate the hat with feathers, sequins, glitter, fabric scraps, and flowers. Punch a hole on either side with the paper punch. Knot lengths of ribbon or yarn through the holes and tie under your chin.

Wink, Wink

All the guests sit in a circle. Each receives a folded slip of paper. Only one paper has an "X" on it. The person who receives it is "It." The object of the game is for "It" to eliminate the others one by one by catching someone's eye and winking at him. That person waits a second, in order to avoid giving "It" away, then announces, "I'm out." Players may guess at any time who is doing the winking. If the guess is correct, the game is over. If the guess is incorrect, the player who made the guess is out.

Favors

Guests can take home the Paper-Plate Party Hats that they made and the Paper-Doily Baskets. (See directions below.) Some other favor ideas are costume jewelry, bow ties, combs, ribbons, key chains, barrettes, wallets, and bubble bath.

Paper-Doily Baskets

You will need round paper doilies, glue, construction paper, and markers. Fold each doily in half. Form it into a cone shape, overlap the edges, and glue them together. Cut out a strip of construction paper. Glue the ends inside the doily for a handle. Write a guest's name on each basket. Fill with candies and set one at each guest's place setting.

Ahoy, Mateys!

Put on pirate hats, eye patches, and bandannas, and climb aboard the Jolly Roger for a pirate party. Who hasn't dreamed of searching for buried treasure on exotic islands? Yo-ho-ho!

Invitations

You will need brown paper grocery bags, markers, and twine. Tear a piece from the grocery bag. On it, use the markers to draw a map to your house. Mark a big "X" where your house is and write on the map "X marks the spot for (your name)'s Pirate Birthday Party!" Include your address, the date and time of the party, and R.S.V.P. and your phone number. Don't forget to tell guests to come dressed as pirates. Crinkle the paper to look like an old map. Roll up the map and tie a piece of twine around it. Hand-deliver the invitations, or mail them in envelopes.

Decorations

Decorate the party area with paper skeletons and black and white balloons and streamers.

Skull-and-Crossbones Place Mats

You will need black and white construction paper, scissors, glue, and a black marker. Cut out a skull and crossbones from white paper, as shown. Glue it onto a sheet of black paper. Using the marker, draw eyes, a nose, a mouth, and a guest's name on the skull. Put one at each place setting.

Treasure Chest Centerpiece

You will need a box, aluminum foil, tape, and lots of costume jewelry or candy, such as foil-covered chocolate or bubble gum coins, jellybeans, etc. Cover the box with the aluminum foil. Set the box in the center of the table and fill it to overflowing with the costume jewelry or candy.

Menu

Veggie and Dip Island

Fill a bowl with dip made from packaged mix and sour cream. Wash a few leafy celery stalks. Insert celery in the dip for palm trees. Surround the bowl with carrot and celery sticks.

Tuna Boats

Butter hot dog buns and lightly toast them in an oven at 450°. Fill the buns with tuna or chicken salad, sprinkle with grated cheese, and bake them until the cheese melts. Remove from oven. Cut cheese slices into "sails," thread them on toothpicks, and insert them into the "boats." Serve warm.

Treasure Chest Cake

Bake a sheet cake, using your favorite mix. Frost the sides with chocolate icing and the top with vanilla icing. Decorate with candy "jewels," such as foil-covered chocolate or bubble gum coins, so the cake looks like an overflowing treasure chest.

Pirate Punch

Serve lemonade with banana slices, pineapple chunks, and orange slices.

Activities

Treasure Hunt

Before the guests arrive, print nine clues on separate slips of paper. Fold them and hide them in their proper hiding places. Start by reading the first clue aloud. The guests follow instructions to the second clue, and so on until they find the last note telling where the treasure is hidden. The treasure is a sealed cardboard box full of wrapped party favors, one for each guest.

Snatch the Flag

Each guest hangs a bandanna out of his or her pocket or waistband. The object of the game is for each person to snatch the other players' "flags" without losing his or her own. Anyone who loses his or her "flag" is out. The winner is the last person to have a "flag."

Yo-Ho-Ho

The guests sit in a circle. One person stands in the middle, throws a bandanna into the air, and starts laughing. Everyone else laughs, too, until the bandanna hits the floor. At that moment there should be complete silence, and anyone who laughs is out.

Pirate's Earring

The guests stand in a circle, hands behind their backs. One person is "It" and stands in the center. Another person has a ring and walks around the outside of the circle, pretending to give the ring to one of the players. He or she finally gives the ring to someone. "It" has three guesses as to who really has the ring.

Treasure Chest

Place several objects in a shallow box. Show the box to the guests for one minute, then remove it. For younger guests, take out one object, then return the "treasure chest" to them. They must guess which object is missing. For older guests, supply each with a piece of paper and a pencil. They must write down as many of the objects as they can remember.

Favors

Guests can take home small bags filled with foil-covered chocolate or bubble gum coins, or shiny pennies. (To make pennies shiny, drop them in a mixture of four tablespoons salt + ½ cup vinegar.) Other suggestions are bandannas or pirate eye patches and hats. (See directions below.)

Pirate Eye Patches

Cut out eye patches from black felt, as shown. Poke a small hole on each side of the patch and thread elastic through so guests can tie the patches around their heads. (You might want to pass out the eye patches, bandannas, and pirate hats at the beginning of the party so guests can wear them.)

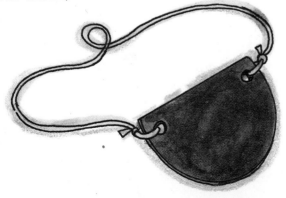

Pirate Hats

You can make these from sheets of newspaper, following the folding directions below.

1. Fold one sheet of newspaper in half.

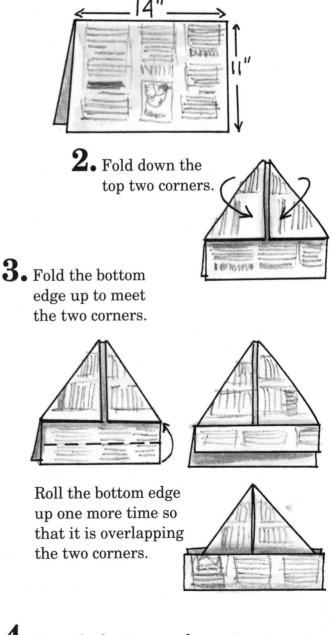

2. Fold down the top two corners.

3. Fold the bottom edge up to meet the two corners.

Roll the bottom edge up one more time so that it is overlapping the two corners.

4. Turn the hat over and repeat step 3 on the other side.

Play Ball!

Are you just wild about baseball? Here's a party to fulfill your baseball dreams. If space permits, let the highlight of the party be a baseball game!

Invitations

You will need construction paper, pictures of baseball players from magazines, scissors, glue, and markers. Fold a piece of construction paper in half. Glue the pictures of baseball players to the front of the card. Inside write "Let's Play Ball!" Include your name, address, the date and time of the party, and R.S.V.P. and your phone number. If you're going to play a baseball game, be sure to tell your guests to dress appropriately. Also, ask them to bring photos for Make-Your-Own Baseball Cards.

Decorations

Decorate the party area with baseball posters and team pennants. Cover the table with newspaper sports pages. Set the Baseball Diamond Birthday Cake in the center of the table for a centerpiece.

Baseball Glove Place Mats

You will need brown and white construction paper, a pencil, scissors, a paper punch, brown yarn, glue, and markers. Trace a mitt shape on the brown paper and cut it out. Punch holes in the mitt, as shown, and lace the yarn through the holes. Cut out a baseball from white paper and glue it to the mitt. Decorate with markers.

Baseball Diamond Birthday Cake

Bake a sheet cake, using your favorite mix. When it has cooled, cut off a portion on one side of the cake so that it is square. Frost the cake with green icing to make a baseball field. (Add a few drops of green food coloring to vanilla icing to make green icing.) Place four small square cookies or pieces of candy in the corners to make the bases. Top with baseball figures.

Menu

Have bowls of popcorn and peanuts available for guests to munch on while playing baseball and other games. For the main meal serve hot dogs, carrot and celery "bats," and lemonade. For the grand finale, bring on the Ice-Cream Baseballs and Baseball Diamond Birthday Cake. (See following recipes.)

Ice-Cream Baseballs

Set baking cups on a baking sheet. Scoop vanilla ice cream into balls and put them in the baking cups. Decorate with red or brown icing squeezed from a tube to look like the seams of a baseball. Store the ice-cream baseballs in the freezer until it is time to eat them.

Activities

If you live near a park or have a large yard, the highlight of the party can be a baseball or tee ball game.

Make-Your-Own Baseball Cards

You will need cardboard, scissors, photographs, glue, and markers. Tell guests to bring photos of themselves (preferably playing baseball). (Or photograph each guest with an instant camera.) Cut out a 3-inch by 4-inch rectangle from the cardboard. Guests glue their photos in the center of the cards, then decorate with their names, the names of their favorite teams, and the team's colors. On the back, guests write in their "statistics."

Baseball Beanbag Toss

Set up a mini baseball diamond, with boxes at each base. Each player stands on home plate and gets three chances to toss a beanbag on the bases. First base is worth one point, second base is worth three points (since it's a longer distance), and third base is worth two points. Guests can play as many rounds as they want. The player with the most points is the winner.

Over-Under Relay Race

Guests divide into two teams and form two rows. The first player on each team holds a ball. At the word "Go!" the first player passes the ball over her head to the second player, who passes it between his legs to the third player. The ball is passed over and under the entire length of the row. The last player to receive the ball runs to the head of the line and starts the ball in motion again. Play continues until the players are back in their original positions and the first player is holding the ball. The team that finishes first wins.

The Singing Ball

One player leaves the room. While she is gone, a baseball is hidden. When the player returns, she must find the ball. The other players will help her out by singing as she looks for the ball. The closer she gets to the ball, the louder everyone will sing. The farther away she gets from the ball, the softer everyone will sing. A good song to sing during this game is "Take Me Out to the Ball Game."

Call Ball

Guests form a circle, with one person in the middle. That person tosses a ball high, while calling out the name of another player. That player tries to catch the ball before it hits the ground. If he does, that player becomes the ball-tosser. If the player does not catch the ball, the first ball-tosser continues to toss the ball and call out names until a player catches the ball.

Favors

Guests can take home the baseball cards they made during the party. Some other ideas are baseball cards, team pennants, baseball caps, baseballs autographed by all the guests, and baseball storybooks.

Wild, Wild West Party

Howdy, pardners! Get out your jeans, boots, and cowboy hats, and come on out for a galloping good time at a Wild West party. Indoors or outdoors, you can create a great Wild West setting, using all the ideas below.

Invitations

You will need construction paper, twine, scissors, glue, and markers. Fold a piece of construction paper in half. Form a lasso out of twine and glue to the front of the invitation. Using the markers, in the center of the lasso write "We're rounding up everyone for (your name)'s Wild, Wild West Birthday Party!" Inside the invitation, write the date and time, your address, R.S.V.P., and your phone number, and "Please wear your cowboy and cowgirl clothes!"

Decorations

Create a Wild West scene by cutting out cactuses, horses, cattle, and a fence from cardboard or poster board. Paint the figures and prop them up around the party area. Set up tents and hay bales for seats (if the party is outside).

Cover the party table with a red-and-white-checked tablecloth. For napkins, roll up a bandanna, tie with a piece of twine, and set at each place setting. Set a Sheriff's Badge Cookie (see directions, next page) with a guest's name on it at each place setting.

Use the Corral Cake as a table centerpiece, or create a village of log cabins with toy logs.

WE'RE ROUNDING UP EVERYONE FOR TOMMY'S WILD, WILD WEST BIRTHDAY PARTY!

Menu

If your family owns camping gear, you can serve the party food in your camping dishes. Or you can serve the food in aluminum or metal pie tins.

Sheriff's Badge Cookies

Prepare sugar cookie dough, using your favorite mix. Cut the cookies into star shapes with a cookie cutter and bake. Let cool. Frost with icing, and sprinkle with colored sugar crystals. Write each guest's name on a cookie with icing squeezed from a tube.

Chili-Corn Bread Cups

Make your favorite chili recipe. While the chili is cooking, prepare corn bread batter and pour into foil bake cups, one tablespoon per cup. Bake at 400° for 10 minutes. Remove from the oven and spoon chili on top of the corn bread. Top with grated cheese and serve warm.

Corral Cake

Bake a sheet cake, using your favorite mix Mix a few drops of green food coloring into vanilla icing, and frost the cake. Make a fence out of ice-cream sticks to go around the edge of the cake. Top the cake with cowboy, horse, and cattle figures.

Activities

Rattlesnake

Guests sit in a circle. When the music begins, pass around a stuffed snake. When the music stops, the player caught holding the snake is out.

Potato Toppers

Just before the party begins, bake one potato for each guest in a 400° oven for one hour. Keep potatoes warm in the oven. Prepare the toppings and arrange them on a buffet table. Place each potato in a bowl and have guests select their own toppings. Suggested toppings: ground beef cooked in taco seasoning, crumbled bacon, butter or margarine, grated Cheddar or Parmesan cheese, sour cream, and crumbled tortilla chips.

Panning for Gold

Fill a plastic wading pool with sand. Mix some shiny pennies into the sand. (You can make the pennies shiny by dropping them in a mixture of four tablespoons salt + ½ cup vinegar.) Each guest gets a chance to pan for "gold" using a pie tin or strainer.

Campfire Sing-Along

If you are having your party outdoors, guests can sit around a real campfire to sing songs. *(Adult supervision is recommended.)* If you have a friend who can play the guitar, harmonica, or any other instrument, ask if he or she can lead the sing-along. Some suggested songs are "Home on the Range," "Clementine," and "Oh! Susanna."

Cattle Roundup

Before the party begins, set up an obstacle course. Some suggested obstacles are chairs, tables, trees, bushes, and large boxes. Divide the guests into two teams and demonstrate the course. Provide each team with a broom and a balloon. At the signal "Go!" the first member of each team must herd their balloon "cattle" through the obstacle course with the broom. If the balloon bursts, the player must return to the starting line, get a new balloon, and begin the course again. Once finished, the first player hands the broom to the second player, and so on. The first team to finish herding its "cattle" wins.

You can end the evening by toasting marshmallows over the campfire or grill. *(Adult supervision is recommended.)*

Favors

Guests can take home the napkin bandannas and the Sheriff's Badge Cookies. Some other ideas are cowboy hats or small plastic cowboy or horse figures.

If you have an instant camera, you can take a picture of each guest in his or her cowboy or cowgirl attire. Frame each picture in a "Wanted" frame (directions above).

"Wanted" Picture Frame

You will need cardboard, a ruler, brown paper lunch bags, scissors, glue, markers, and photos. Cut out a 5-inch by 7-inch piece of cardboard. Cut out a 3-inch by 4½-inch square from the center. Crumple up a lunch bag, then smooth it out. Lay the cardboard frame on the bag and trace around the outside and inside of the frame. Cut out the lunch bag frame and glue it on top of the cardboard frame. Squeeze a thin line of glue around the front edge of the photo. Center the frame over the photo and press down in the glued area. (You may want to pile several heavy books on top of the frame until it dries.) Using the markers, write "Wanted" at the top of the frame. Make up a name for each guest, such as Kevin the Kid or Calamity Cathy, and write it at the bottom of the frame.

$4.95 U.S.
$6.99 Canada

It's your birthday,

so plan a party with one of these themes in mind:

Beach Party

Haunted House

Outer Space

Carnival

Under the Sea

Safari

Olympics Festival

Tea Party

Pirates

Baseball

Wild, Wild West

All the easy-to-follow instructions are here to create the atmosphere for these party themes with festive invitations, decorations, menus, activities, and favors. Have a fun-filled and memorable birthday bash!

Boyds Mills Press

Distributed by St. Martin's Press

ISBN 1-878093-38-X

9 781878 093387

50495